USBORNE HOTSHOTS

BIKES

USBORNE HOTSHOTS
BIKES

Janet Cook and Jessica Kent

Edited by Lisa Miles and Mandy Ross
Designed by Helen Westwood

Illustrated by Kim Raymond and Kuo Kang Chen
Photography by Mike Powell, Allsport USA

Series editor: Judy Tatchell
Series designer: Ruth Russell

CONTENTS

Choosing a bike

If you are buying a bike, think about what kind of riding you want to do. Mountain bikes are strong and sturdy, designed for rough ground. Racing bikes are light and responsive for streamlined speed on roads. Other types of road bikes combine features from mountain and racing bikes, for safe riding around town, or on easy tracks and trails. These bikes are sometimes called hybrids.

Below is a picture of a mountain bike, showing its special features. It can climb slippery slopes and cope with ditches and potholes, water, sand and mud. On the opposite page is a racing bike so you can see how it differs from a mountain bike.

Frame is smaller than a racing bike's to make it stronger, safer and easier to control.

Usually more gears (up to 24) than on a racing bike to allow for varied conditions. Derailleur gears, shown here, are used on both mountain and racing bikes.

Most mountain bikes have a padded saddle, to make them more comfortable to ride on rough surfaces.

Top tube is lower than a racing bike's, so it is less dangerous if you fall.

Pedals have jagged edges for extra grip.

Bottom of the frame is higher than a racing bike's, so it clears the bumps.

Thick, knobby tires provide a good grip for off-road riding.

About racing bikes

A racing bike is designed for lightness and speed on roads and race tracks. The frame is made of a rigid, light material such as alloy steel tubing, to make steering and pedaling more responsive at speed.

Drop handlebars

Drop handlebars and a narrow saddle let you lean forward in a streamlined position. Skinny wheels and tires can travel over a hard surface faster than a mountain bike's thick, knobby ones.

Some mountain bikes have handlebar extensions like these, for comfort and extra control. Racing bikes have lower, curved handlebars instead, called drop handlebars (see above).

The gear levers are positioned so that you can change gear without letting go of the handlebars.

Brakes. Types vary, but cantilever brakes, like these, are most common. They are strong and easy to maintain. Racing bikes have lighter, caliper brakes.

Wheels are 66cm (26in) in diameter, smaller than on a racing bike. They are fatter, too, for strength and grip.

Chunky forks for maximum strength.

Always wear a helmet that fits well.

Getting started

It is important to make sure you are safe and comfortable when you go out on a ride. Below are some simple checks to make before you set off, and on the right, a basic tool kit to carry with you, in case you need to make urgent repairs while you are out.

You can save money – and get a lot of satisfaction – by taking care of your bike yourself. For more detailed information, find a bike maintenance book in your local library or bookstore.

If the brake levers are stiff, spray some lubricant inside, where the cables join the levers. (You can buy lubricant in most bike shops.)

Check that all wheel bolts are tight or quick-release levers are locked.

Worn brake blocks don't work effectively. Replacing them is cheap and easy to do.

Make sure your brake cables are not frayed.

Check your tire pressure. On roads, tires should be pumped up hard. Softer tires grip better off road.*

Check tires for signs of wear, to protect the inner tube.

If the wheels are rubbing unevenly against the brake blocks, you should ask a mechanic to check the spokes' tension.

Early in the ride, run through all your gears to make sure they change smoothly.

Oil the chain if it is squeaky. Too much oil attracts dirt, so use as little as you can.

* Tire pressures on page 30.

Basic tool kit

Wrap these items up in a cloth and take them on each ride. You can clean your hands with the cloth after making repairs. Tie the kit behind your saddle or under the top tube, or take it in a saddle pouch.

Spoke key for adjusting spokes or removing broken ones

Screwdriver

Allen keys to fit nuts of different sizes

Pump

Adjustable wrench

Chain tool

Swiss army knife

Spare inner tube

Tire levers

Flat repair kit

Pliers

Cycling gear

Uncomfortable clothes can make riding miserable. Shorts or a tracksuit and tennis shoes are practical. You can also buy special cycling gear, designed for comfort, visibility and reduced wind-resistance.

Helmet

Gloves

Bright, skin-tight shirt

Shorts with padded crotch lining

Shoes

Shoes with stiff soles are the most efficient. They transmit all your pedaling power straight to the pedal.

Protection

Cycling glasses protect your eyes from dust and grit. Choose ones with ultra-violet filters.

It is vital that your helmet fits correctly. Check by strapping it on and shaking your head. Both micro-shell and hard-shell helmets give good protection, but micro-shell helmets are lighter. Wide vents at the front keep your head cool.

Mountain bike boot

All-around cycling shoe

Micro-shell helmet

Hard-shell helmet

7

Bike basics

Good braking and gear-changing techniques will help you to ride safely and use your energy efficiently. Follow the advice on these two pages until these basic skills become good habits.

A correct riding position is important. The pictures here show the most efficient and comfortable positions.

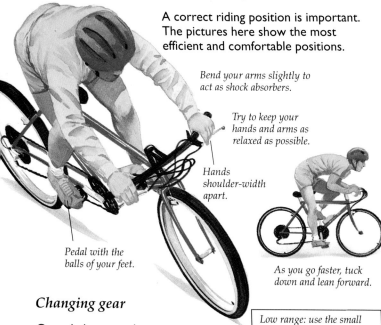

Bend your arms slightly to act as shock absorbers.

Try to keep your hands and arms as relaxed as possible.

Hands shoulder-width apart.

Pedal with the balls of your feet.

As you go faster, tuck down and lean forward.

Changing gear

Gears help you to keep a constant pedal rate (cadence) – ideally a brisk 80-90 turns or revolutions per minute. There are three ranges of gears (see boxes on the right).

Sprockets

Chainwheels

Keep pedaling as you change gear, but gently ease off the pressure on the pedals.

Low range: use the small chainwheel and the two or three largest sprockets. For climbing hills.

Middle range*: use the middle-sized chainwheel and sprockets. For easy hills or cycling into strong winds.

High range: use the large chainwheel and the two or three smallest sprockets. For riding at top speed.

*For a middle range with only two chainwheels, use the large chainwheel with the larger sprockets, or the small one with the smaller sprockets.

Turning

Use your weight to help you turn tight corners with ease, as shown here. Try this in a flat, quiet area first!

1. Approach the turn just fast enough to avoid wobbling.

2. Lean into the turn. This movement should come from the hips.

Braking

It is easy to skid when riding off-road. Careful braking reduces the risk.

1. Keep your weight far back, and ease on the back brake.

2. Then make gentle pulls on the front brake (called feathering).

3. Now turn the handlebars as smoothly as you can.

4. Bring the handlebars and your body level to go straight again.

Falling off

If you can't avoid a fall when you skid or hit an obstacle, this technique may reduce the chance of hurting yourself.

1. If the front wheel catches an obstacle, the bike stops but your body keeps going forward.

2. Release one hand and foot to steady your fall. Your other hand eases the bike to the ground.

3. Keep your arms and legs relaxed to absorb the shock, and bring your body to a sitting position.

Uphill and downhill

Reaching the top of a very steep hill is extremely satisfying – and the downhill ride can be exciting too. Here are some tips to get you up and down safely.

Climbing technique

The most efficient way to climb is to stay on the saddle in a low gear for as long as you can. Your tires get a better grip this way. Pedaling out of the saddle (see below) gives you a burst of power, but is more tiring.

Sitting. Lean forward for more controlled steering.

Standing. Keep your weight over the pedals.

For extra force, stand up and move your body weight from side to side as you pedal. The bike should rock slightly.

Uphill gear changing

Try to pedal at the same rate throughout a climb. Do this by changing down early, before your cadence drops and you start to struggle.

Steering around obstacles

Steering around obstacles while going downhill demands careful control. It is important to keep your speed down.

1. Keep your weight over the back of the bike, and pull gently on both brakes to slow down.

2. Lean your body in the direction of the turn, and ease the handlebars around gently. Jerky turns can cause skids.

3. Keep the pedal nearest the obstacle high, to avoid it catching on the obstacle.

4. Finally, lean out to bring the bike upright again.

Carrying your bike

Some hills are too uneven or slippery to push your bike up. Here is the most efficient way to carry your bike until you can get back on the saddle again.

Support the top tube on your right shoulder.

Hold the handlebar with your left hand.

Downhill off-road

Going downhill, the trick is to keep your weight low and to the back of the bike, as shown here. Lowering the saddle will make this easier. If you lean forward, you are likely to be catapulted over the handlebars.

Keep your knees bent and relaxed. They will then act as shock absorbers.

Stick your backside out.

Press down firmly on the pedals and keep them level with each other.

Tricks and stunts

These tricks and stunts should impress your friends – and you might find them useful for getting over obstacles such as fallen logs, holes and ditches. You may find you need a lot of practice!

Wheelies

Learn how to do these in a safe place, wearing protective clothing such as elbow and knee pads and, of course, a helmet.

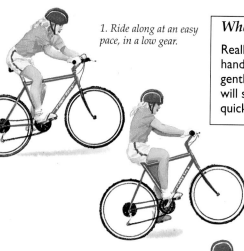

1. Ride along at an easy pace, in a low gear.

Wheelie tip

Really yank at the handlebars. If you are too gentle, the front wheel will scarcely rise, and will quickly fall down again.

2. Bring your weight directly over the point where the back wheel touches the ground.

3. Pull the handlebars sharply up and back. Push down hard on the pedals.

Uphill wheelies

To avoid toppling back doing wheelies uphill, bend your arms and lower your chest as you lift the handlebars. This is called down-unweighting. Don't try wheelies on a steep hill.

4. Bring your body weight forward to recover.

Log hop

A log hop is an extension of a wheelie. After lifting the front wheel, you raise the back one too. Use the log hop to avoid damaging your bike or crashing when you need to get over an obstacle.

1. Get a good speed going to make it over the obstacle. Lift the handlebars as if you were doing a wheelie.

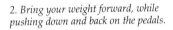

2. Bring your weight forward, while pushing down and back on the pedals.

3. As the front wheel touches the ground again, the back wheel will rise onto the obstacle.

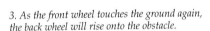

4. Start pedaling so that the bike clears the obstacle, then bring your weight back over the middle of the bike.

If you do the log hop well, you may get over the obstacle without either wheel touching it.

Bunny hop

You can use a bunny hop to get over small obstacles or holes. You jump the bike, raising both wheels at the same time.

1. Try this on level ground at first. Riding slowly, stay out of the saddle and keep your feet level on the pedals.

2. Push down on the pedals and handlebars, then pull the whole bike up with your arms. Keep your weight off the back wheel.

13

Extreme conditions

Mountain bikes are designed to cope with extreme conditions, including water, mud and snow. Here are some techniques you can use on difficult surfaces, whatever kind of bike you ride.

Crossing water

The secret of crossing shallow streams is to pedal extra hard. You need to keep up enough speed, or momentum, to carry you over any rocks or obstacles in your way.

1. Approach the stream as quickly as possible. Lean forward as you enter it.

2. Transfer your weight to the back of the bike, to help get the front wheel over rocks.

3. Keep pedaling if you can, to maintain your balance and momentum.

Mud, snow, sand and ice

Use your common sense on treacherous surfaces. Never cycle in these conditions when other vehicles are around – they could easily skid into you. Keep away from melting ice or deep snow – 10cm (4in) is about the limit.

 In mud and snow, steer smoothly and use low gears. Wear cycling glasses.

 Use low gears in sand to avoid wheels digging in. Steer very gently.

 Avoid ice if at all possible. If you cannot avoid it, go very slowly. If you feel yourself start to skid, steer in the same direction as the skid.

4. Keep your weight over the back wheel as the front wheel comes out of the stream.

Weather watch

Listen to the weather forecast and look out for the signs below to see if rain is coming. Then you can shelter before it arrives.

Red sky first thing in the morning

Low clouds which haven't cleared by noon.

Cumulonimbus clouds, like these, mean storms are coming.

The metal in your bike attracts lightning. If you get caught in a lightning storm, abandon your bike and head for shelter. Avoid high ground or trees. Lightning looks for the shortest route to earth and either of these may be its target.

Road bike techniques

These road bike techniques are fairly basic, but you need to be able to do them automatically and with confidence. This is especially true when you are competing in a race.

Ankling

If you have toeclips or cleats (see below) you can use a technique called ankling to increase your pedaling power. You pull the pedal up with your ankle and foot as well as pushing it down.

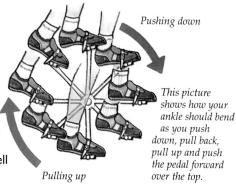

Pushing down

This picture shows how your ankle should bend as you push down, pull back, pull up and push the pedal forward over the top.

Pulling up

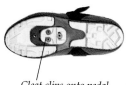

Cleat clips onto pedal

Both toeclips and cleats (tiny quick-release clips on the soles of some cycling shoes) keep your foot securely on the pedal. Cleats are useful because they let you pull up and back on the pedal without your foot slipping off it or out of the toeclip.

Practice tip

Ankling with one leg at a time is good practice. Make sure your cleat or toeclip is fastened securely.

Hold your free foot out of the way so it does not catch the pedal.

Try to keep an even pressure on the pedal all the way around.

Lots of practice with each leg will build up your leg muscles.

Going downhill

Keep your weight back and just off the saddle with your arms almost straight and your pedals level. Control your speed mainly with the back brake.

Climbing

Shift down as you approach a hill, to avoid losing speed half-way up. If you can, stay in the saddle in a low gear, rather than getting off and pushing the bike.

Braking and cornering at high speed

Riding on roads, it is best to use both brakes evenly and as gently as possible to avoid skids. Shift your body weight back and down as you brake, to stabilize the bike. In wet weather, brake rapidly on and off to dry your wheel rims, so the brakes can get a good grip.

If you need to brake to get around a corner, do so as you approach it and not as you go around. Change down in advance so that you can accelerate out of the corner.

On a corner, smooth off the bend to keep your speed up. Check behind, then swing out slightly. Never cross into the opposite lane.

The faster you go, the more you lean into the corner. Stop pedaling and keep the inside pedal high so it does not catch on the ground. Hold your inside knee out from your body for balance.

17

Mountain bike competitions

You don't have to be a top athlete to enter a mountain bike competition. You will be competing against the terrain as well as against other competitors. These two pages show some of the different mountain bike events, and some handy racing tips.

In an observed trial, above, you ride over obstacles while judges watch you. You must try not to touch the ground, fall or stop.

In cross-country racing, you race over a circuit of sharp turns, obstacles to jump, streams, steep hills and so on. The cyclist who gets to the finish line first is the winner. It helps to ride the course before the race if you can.

In hill climbs, you ride up a steep hill over rough ground. The winner has the fastest time or the highest climb.

In downhill races, you ride a winding course down a hair-raising hill. The rider with the best time wins the race.

Fitness tips

Fitness and energy are very important when you are racing. Regular riding and exercise will improve your fitness, stamina and speed.

A balanced diet and lots of fresh food will build up your energy reserves. On the days before the race, eat carbohydrate-rich foods like rice and pasta. There is more about food during the race on page 22.

There is more about food during the race on page 22.

Racing tips

- Make sure your bike is in tip-top condition before the race.

- In mass start events, try to find a place near the front of the group so you don't get held up by slow starters.

- If you want to pass other riders in a mountain bike race, shout to warn them, then wait for them to respond before trying to get past.

- Move over quickly if a racer warns you that he or she is about to pass.

- If you get a flat, fix it as quickly as possible. You can buy small carbon dioxide cartridges which inflate the tire in a few seconds.

Road racing

Speed, fitness and stamina are vital for success in road racing – but so are your tactics. You will learn by observing and experimenting, so enter races even if you don't have much chance of winning.

Closed-circuit races

To avoid dangerous traffic, it is safest for juvenile riders (under the age of 16) to compete in closed-circuit races, or "criteriums", on routes closed to traffic in towns, parks or industrial areas.

Race distances

Juveniles (under 16s) – 6km (10 miles) or 40km (25 miles).

Juniors (16-18s) – between 40-100km (25-62 miles).

Adult riders – usually 100-120km (62-75 miles) but up to 200km (124 miles).

Riding in a pack

You can travel much faster in a pack than as a lone rider. The front rider forges a path through the air stream. By drafting close behind you can travel fast with up to 30% less effort. To share the effort, each rider takes turns at the front – called a paceline.

Riders share the effort by taking turns to keep the speed up.

Competitors help each other like this until the final sprint, when each one will try to get ahead

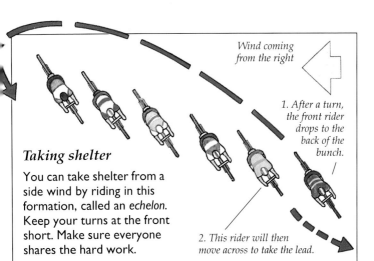

Wind coming from the right

1. After a turn, the front rider drops to the back of the bunch.

Taking shelter

You can take shelter from a side wind by riding in this formation, called an *echelon*. Keep your turns at the front short. Make sure everyone shares the hard work.

2. This rider will then move across to take the lead.

Race tactics

During the race, smaller groups try to pull ahead of the main group. This is called making a break or attacking.

Near the end of a race you need to be in a bunch near the front. There may be a sprint finish. Try to make a lone break at the end and leave the others behind.

Bluffing

If you are feeling the strain of a race, others may be too. Ride confidently and try to hide your discomfort. They may let you pass without a challenge.

Mental preparation

A race is a personal thing. Some riders feel they must calm themselves before an event, while others need to wind themselves up. Over time you will find out what works best for you.

Time trials

A time trial is an all-out race against the clock over a fixed distance. Most take place on the open road, but some are held on cycle tracks. Competitors start at one-minute intervals and follow a marked route, with marshals to direct them at road junctions.

Lightness for speed

You can ride a time trial on any racing bike, but keep it as light as you can. If you can afford them, you can buy special time trial wheels that have fewer spokes to cut down on weight.

Before the race

Time trials, like all races, are demanding, so you need to warm your muscles up before you start. A good way to warm up is to ride to the start if it is not more than an hour's gentle ride away. Then do some stretches, such as touching your toes or side stretches.

Race food

In an event lasting an hour or more, you may "bonk" – when you suddenly feel tired and shaky because you have used up your energy reserves. To avoid this, eat energy-rich snacks regularly as you ride, such as bananas, dried fruit, or a candy bar.

You should start drinking water early in the race, even if you don't feel thirsty. Eat and drink little and often.

During the race

Keep your focus on the road ahead.
Don't look back or you will lose
concentration and speed. Maintain a
steady cadence throughout. Counting your pedal
revolutions can help you strike up a rhythm.

Maintain your effort just below the point at which you
become exhausted. If you go over this limit, you will waste
time slowing down to recover.

Team time trials

In this event, teams of two or
four riders compete over a
course of up to 100km (62
miles). Team members take
turns at the front. The time
registered is that of the second
rider in a team of two, or the
third rider in a team of four.

Starting the time trial

At the start of a time
trial, you need a
helper to hold your
bike up, with you on
it. Have a practice
session with a
friend. They should
hold the saddle at
the back, or stand
beside you holding
the handlebars and
saddle post.

Start with the pedals
at about 11 o'clock
and 5 o'clock. Try to
get a powerful start
without wobbling.

*Keep your head and
body low, and your elbows
tucked in. This helps you
remain as streamlined as
possible.*

23

More cycling events

There are plenty of different cycling events, each one demanding different skills and techniques. Events are held by cycling clubs and organizations. Your local library will help you to find your nearest club.

Track racing

This is the fastest form of cycle racing. The track is designed for top speed, with steeply banked ends to help you corner as fast as possible. The smooth surface helps speed too.

You must not cycle below the gauge line.

Track markings for different races

Start and finish lines for Pursuit races (see opposite)

Riders try to stay close to the gauge line, as it is the shortest and fastest route around the track.

A track bike has neither brakes nor gears, to make it as light as possible. It has no freewheel mechanism, so you slow down by slowing the rate at which the pedals turn.

Olympic cycle tracks measure either 250m (273.3yd) or 333.3m (364.5yd) along the gauge line.

Triathlons and biathlons

A triathlon includes three sports – cycling, swimming and running. The competitors have to do a course of each one, without a break in between. In a biathlon, competitors run, then cycle, then run again.

Track races

Some velodromes, as bicycle tracks are known, have special nights for beginners. They will lend you a bike and give you some coaching. Here are some track races you might find.

Match sprints

In the early laps of a match sprint, the two riders try to save energy for the final sprint. They use crafty tactics, such as dropping speed suddenly to force the other to overtake, or even balancing on the bike at a complete standstill!

Toward the end of the race, each rider must try to gauge the right moment to accelerate into an explosive sprint to the finishing line.

Pursuits

Two riders start on opposite sides of the track and the rider who either closes the gap, or completes the course first, wins.

Devil take the hindmost

At the end of each lap, the last rider goes out of the race. Just two or three riders are left for the final lap. They sprint to finish this lap.

The bike has no brakes or gears, so you have to use your feet to slow down at corners.

The bike has a lightweight frame and knobby tires.

Cycle speedway

This fast and furious event is run on circuits between 50-100m (55-110yd) long. The race is usually four laps and lasts around 45 seconds. Four riders compete. The aim is to get into the lead on the first corner and then stay in the lead!

City riding

Riding your bike in a city presents different hazards to those off-road or out of town. Your bike is smaller and quieter than other traffic, so do everything you can to draw attention to yourself. Use your lights when visibility is bad, such as when it is raining, as well as after dark. Here are some things to help you be seen.

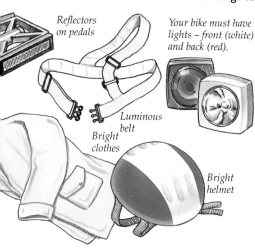

Reflectors on pedals

Your bike must have lights – front (white) and back (red).

Luminous belt

Bright clothes

Bright helmet

Locking up

To avoid theft, always lock your bike up, and take any removable parts with you. Fold a note of your address inside the saddle post. If your bike is in the garage, never leave the garage door open.

Know your route

It is important to know where you are heading. Trying to map-read at the side of the road or following street signs prevents you from concentrating on the traffic. Before your ride, take the time to study your route on a detailed map. You may find it helpful to write yourself brief notes, then memorize them.

* North up City Road
* 4th right Hoskins Street
* 2nd left Park Row
* 3rd left Kestrel Street
* 1st right Cherry Tree Road
* 2nd right East Welling Avenue

Cycle the route slowly, looking out for danger areas. You will then be fully prepared if you have to go that way again.

Traffic hazards

Cycling in traffic requires you to cope with situations where other people act stupidly. Here are some things to look out for.

People opening car doors or pulling out right in front of you.

Motorcyclists (especially dispatch riders) swerving in and out of cars.

Drivers cutting in front of you as they turn into a driveway or a side road.

Safety tips

- Remember always to protect your head with a helmet.
- Keep looking behind. It's easier to duck your head down to look back than twist your neck around.
- Keep your hands on the brake levers, always ready to brake.
- Watch out in rain. You will lose a lot of braking power.
- Don't jump traffic lights or cycle the wrong way up one-way streets. Remember to use hand signals.

Potholes

The best way to deal with potholes is to steer around them. The flow of traffic, however, may make this impossible. Here's how to ride over them safely – or else do a bunny hop (see page 13).

1. Slow down as you approach. Stand on the pedals with bent knees.

2. Keep the bike straight and pull the handlebars up as you go over the pothole.

3. Increase your speed again once the back wheel is clear.

Injuries

Here are some ways to treat minor injuries, plus some tips on how to avoid them. For more serious injuries, always see your doctor.

Minor injuries

Deal with any injury as soon as possible. Clean cuts and grazes with warm water and an antiseptic cream or lotion. Cover the area to protect it from dust and dirt.

You can treat bruises with an ice pack. You can buy these from drug stores, or you can even use a pack of frozen peas! Keep a thin towel between the ice pack and your skin to avoid ice burns. Hold the pack in place for 20 minutes.

First aid kit

Take a first aid kit with you on long rides.

Large triangular bandage
(for slings)
Sterile dressings
Roll of bandage
Elastic bandage
Bandaids
Aspirin
Antiseptic lotion
Damp wipes
Insect repellant
Scissors
Tweezers
Safety pins

Common problems

• **Cramps** Avoid cramps by warming up (see below). Treat it by pressing hard into the thick part of the muscle.

• **Saddle sores** Use padded cycling shorts. Treat the sores by bathing with warm water and a cleanser, not soap. If necessary, stop riding to let sores heal.

• **Painful joints** Check your riding position. Your arms, legs and back should never be fully extended. See a doctor if pain continues.

• **Numb hands or feet** Shift the position of your hands on the handlebars more often, and loosen your toeclips if you use them.

Warming up and down

You can avoid aching muscles by doing a few light exercises before and after your ride. Try some easy stretches or toe touches. Always start your ride gently and gradually build up. At the end of the ride ease off the pace to warm down.

Buying a bike

If you decide to buy a brand-new bike, try to find a good specialist shop that will give sound advice and also backup mechanical help.

Buying second-hand can be a really good deal. Ask an experienced rider for advice before you agree on a price. Below are some major signs of damage or wear to look out for. If you are confident the bike is roadworthy, take it for a test ride.

Damaged or crooked forks. The top of the forks should be in line with the front part of the frame, not bent back. Check by holding a ruler against them.

Bent wheels. Spin to see if they run straight, checking from the front and the side.

Dented rims. Also check that spokes are taut.

Bent frame. Look along the bike from back to front. Also check for dents where the tubes join at the front of the bike.

Worn teeth on the chainwheels and sprockets.

Check for good quality butted tubing (thicker and stronger at the joints). Flick with your finger. The note should change as you go down the tube.

Checking the fit

Never buy a bike that doesn't fit you. It could do lasting damage to your back or joints. Check these points.

1. Sit on the saddle. Your leg should be slightly bent when the pedal is at its lowest position.

2. Can you reach the handlebars with your elbows slightly bent? The handlebars should be level with the saddle, or as much as 5cm (2in) lower.

3. Stand astride the bike. There should be at least 3-5cm (1-2in) between your crotch and the top tube, and even more for a mountain bike — between 6-15cm (2½-6in).

29

Maintenance tips

Your bike will run better and last longer if you take good care of it. After a ride, give it a quick clean. Then clean your bike thoroughly two or three times a year. For more tips, look in a good bike maintenance book.

After-ride clean

1. Remove mud using water and a brush or sponge. Keep dirty water away from moving parts like the hubs, pedals and bottom bracket, to avoid damaging the bearings (steel balls) inside.

2. Wipe the bike with one towel. Clean the chain and moving parts with lubricant and the other towel, avoiding brakes and rims.

You will need

Garden hose or buckets of water

2 clean old towels

Soft brush or sponge

Spray lubricant (available from a hardware store)

Flat repair

You will need a flat repair kit and a bucket of water, if available. Read the repair kit instructions.

1. Remove the wheel. Starting opposite the valve, remove one side of the tire from the rim.

2. Remove and inflate inner tube. Listen for a hiss, or put it in water and watch for bubbles.

3. Use sandpaper to roughen area. Blow away dust. Apply glue. Leave for two minutes.

4. Stick on the repair patch. Let it dry for three minutes. Check inside the tire for grit or nails.

5. Start with the valve. Replace tube, then tire, on the rim. When it is tucked in, pump tire up.*

* Tire pressure: for road riding, 80psi or 5.6 bars (too hard to depress with thumb); for off-road riding, 45psi or 3.2 bars (softer, but still hard to the touch). If you have no pressure gauge, you can ask to have your tire pressure checked at a bike shop.

Thorough clean

1. Place your bike on a repair stand or upside-down on a towel. Remove the wheels.

2. Break the chain with a chain tool, put it in a shallow tray and cover it with turpentine. Scrub it with the toothbrush and leave it to soak in clean turpentine.

3. Wipe the chainwheels with a towel. Clean the freewheel sprockets with a stiff brush.

4. Turn the frame the right way up and rest on its forks. Mix hot water and detergent in a bucket, and wash and clean the frame and wheels with a soft brush. Rinse with a hose. Avoid the bearings (see page 30).

5. Remove any rust from the frame with steel wool. Touch up with paint and allow several hours to dry. Then wax and polish the frame with a rag.

6. Hold the chain over the tray and let the spirit drip dry. Turn the frame upside down and replace wheels. Put the chain on and join with a chain tool.

You will need

Garden hose

Bucket

Shallow metal tray

3 rags or old towels

Stiff brush

Soft brush

Old toothbrush

Liquid detergent

Hot water

Turpentine*

Car wax*

Steel wool (medium texture)*

Chain tool**

Touch-up paint**

Spray lubricant*

Wrench (if wheels aren't quick-release)

7. Turn the bike the right way up. Spray lubricant on the chain, cable stops, gears and brake pivots. Avoid getting any on the wheel rims or brake blocks.

Yearly overhaul

If you ride a lot, once a year you should dismantle your bike to clean and lubricate it.

You should also replace worn parts. Ask an experienced cyclist to help you.

*Available from a hardware store   **Available from a bike shop*

Index

Additional photography by Allsport USA (19 all); David Cannon, Allsport UK (16 bottom, 22); Muddy Fox (4-5); Stockfile (16 top).

This book is based on material previously published in Usborne Superskills: Mountain Bikes and Racing Bikes.

First published in 1996 by Usborne Publishing Ltd, Usborne House, 83-85 Saffron Hill, London EC1N 8RT, England.

Copyright © Usborne Publishing Ltd 1990, 1996.
First published in America August 1996. AE